MPREG DELIGHT

Non Shifter MPREG MM Romance

Michael Levi

ISBN: 9798406624791
Imprint: Independently published

2nd edition

Cover design by: Michael Levi

CONTENTS

CHAPTER 1

I was a simple resident of an isolated village in California. The year was 1870, and I loved the place where I lived, even though I'd been by myself ever since my wife died.

The village itself was pretty small, and the population had been decreasing by a bit every couple of years. There were only 54 of us living there, and we were all very close. We all knew each other's darkest secrets.

Ever since my wife passed away, more often than not I caught myself ogling some of the guys in the village. About ten years ago, they were small and no more than a passing thought in my mind. Now, they were bigger and, dare I say it, handsome and pretty virile.

They grew up fast, and now they looked like proper men. They had it all. They were strong, confident, and dominant. They almost made me envious of them, but I knew I was on top.

About four months ago, I managed to get laid with one of them. His name was Johnny, and he was perfect. A slender body, blond hair, a face that could make anyone melt on the inside, very red lips, and a thick accent that was like music to my ears.

He was just a bit shorter than I was, but the most noticeable difference between us was the overall size of our bodies. He still needed to work way more often at the ranch to get to my size. Working on the farm was hard and demanding. I was able to haul the guy with just one arm the first night we fucked.

The night we had together in my home was fantastic, but we knew we couldn't tell anyone. People in the village didn't take too kindly to man-on-man action. I could understand their feelings towards that, but I'd always wanted more freedom.

Ever since that night together with Johnny, my belly grew huge. Initially, I thought that it was thanks to me drinking too much at the local saloon, but that couldn't be. I began to drink less beer since then, but my stomach kept on growing.

The worst started to happen a month or two after that night with Johnny. I began to feel tired and dizzy. The symptoms of pregnancy became more and more common, but I refused to believe that I was pregnant.

I mean, really, men don't get pregnant, right? The symptoms kept on popping up, but I kept on telling myself that they'd go away one day.

I went to the doctor in a larger, nearby village, and he also couldn't explain what it was that I was going through.

There was only one other option I could take to find a solution to my problem. People in the village recommended me a nearby curator – or witch, as some liked to describe her. I decided I had nothing to lose, and so I packed up my stuff in a bag and readied the horse to get there tomorrow.

CHAPTER 2

I picked up the bag and put it on the horse. Artax was a good companion. Never once did he do something I didn't want from him. He was fast and strong on the roads, and he's been with me for several years.

The road to the curator's house was a long one. It was also infamous for bandit ambushes, but I didn't have any problems with that while I traversed the road on my way to the curator's house.

The house where the woman lived was falling apart. The walls and the roof were dotted with holes and flaking paint.

I knocked on the front door and then heard some noises coming from inside the house.

The woman who opened the door was very old. She seemed to be about sixty years of age, but I could feel she wasn't a defenseless woman. The stuffed animals and hunting trophies inside the place told me she could deal with bandits easily. I made sure to keep that in mind so that I didn't piss her off.

"What do you want?" She barked.

"I heard you are a curator. I've been feeling nauseous and, sometimes, I puke. I think it's because my belly is bigger now. Can you explain to me what's been happening to me?"

She grunted and looked down at my belly. The look on her face told me she had an idea that could explain what was going on with me.

"Alright, come inside and sit on that chair," the curator said, adding, "and you can call me Marjory."

I walked around in her house and hung my hat on the wall. I sat on the chair and watched her as she worked on some vials on the table. She picked up some herbs and made a concoction.

Then, she said, "Drink this." I did as she asked of me. The flavor of the liquid was horrible, but I heard good things about her. I trusted her work.

"Now, take your shirt off. I need to feel the belly."

I did as she commanded. She looked at my big belly and kneeled in front of me.

I got a bit turned on at that moment. I'd had many women – and a young man – kneel in front of me. Usually, they would go for my rock-hard cock, but Marjory had something else to do.

She put her hand on my belly and I felt how cold it was, even though we were in the middle of a very hot Summer. Then, she put her ear next to my stomach, trying to catch any noise coming from there.

She got up and said, "Okay, now take off your pants and lie on my bed. Then, open your ass so that I can take a look inside your rectum."

Wait, what? This old fart wants to check my ass out?

The look on my face showed her how surprised I was at that demand. I then asked, "Why do you want to do that?"

The curator looked annoyed at my question and then said, "Why do you think I asked that of you? Why did you come here? I need to take a look there to confirm a suspicion of mine. Trust me when I say I don't enjoy this one bit."

With the way she said it, I had to obey her. I took off my pants and headed to her bed. I lied on it and spread my legs for her.

Marjory kneeled behind me and probed my anus with her finger. I felt a bit turned on again. I remembered some naughty details from when Johnny penetrated my hole with his fat cock.

Minutes later, Marjory got up and asked me to get dressed. "I know what's happening with you, cowboy," she said with an enigmatic and terrifying look on her face.

Once I put my shirt and pants on, I walked to where the curator was. She looked deeply into my eyes and I braced myself for the bad news. I was already thinking she was going to tell me I was about to die or something like that.

"You are..." I closed my eyes as I expected the very bad news to come from her mouth, "pregnant. You've been like that for a couple of months already."

I opened my eyes in a heartbeat. Pregnant? Me? But that's impossible!

Marjory seemed to know I didn't believe her words, "I know that you don't believe it because you think that men can't get pregnant. Well, in my experience, some men can."

I tried to refute her words, but I could only open and close my mouth. I couldn't think of what to say to her. She was the expert and was confirming something that had been in my head for a very long time.

Marjory continued her explanation, "Men who get pregnant usually can give birth to healthy babies. You can do that as well, but there's one condition."

Hearing those words from her made me snap back to reality. I was thinking about what my life was going to be like. Having a baby, feeding him or her, and trying to hide them from the other villagers because they couldn't know... My life would be a mess.

"What should I do?" I asked the curator.

"First, you need to find the father of the child. Then, you should explain to him the situation. Try to be very calm and attentive. He might not take it as well as you have."

I definitely wasn't taking that fact well, but the old woman was right about finding the father. I already knew who he was. There was only one man I'd had sex with in my life: Johnny.

He was still living in the village. He was barely a man himself and I imagined he wasn't going to take the news well. He didn't have the mental fortitude for that. He was still living with his parents and his dream was to visit the east coast. It was a dream unlikely to come true in his life, but he was an inexperienced young man, after all.

"I think I know who the father is, Marjory. Here's your payment. I'll be on my way. I need to head back to my village."

I bid farewell and headed back home. I was about to have a full day tomorrow. Meeting Johnny again was not going to be easy.

CHAPTER 3

I got home yesterday feeling exhausted, both mentally and physically. The ride back home felt longer than it really was because I kept thinking about being pregnant, Johnny, and the baby.

How was I going to tell him about what happened? How was he going to deal with his parents? It was obvious to me that they couldn't know what was happening and I was hoping Johnny would understand where I was coming from.

I woke up and looked at myself in the mirror. *Still in good shape at forty years of age*, I thought. I was one of the tallest men in the village, had a nice beard, short black hair, and hazel eyes that most girls usually complimented.

I got dressed and headed outside. The village looked busy at around 8 AM. A lot of people there got up early to begin their work and take care of their children. The saloon was already open and some guests were already inside.

I walked by the saloon and looked inside the building. I spotted Johnny in there, chugging a glass of beer and beaming. I didn't want to spoil his moment, but there was no better occasion to talk to him.

I entered the place and approached the young man. I put one hand on his shoulder and he looked at me. Surprised, he could barely blink. It had been months since the last time I spoke with him. I didn't blame him for having that reaction.

"Johnny, we need to talk... in private."

It took him a couple of seconds to respond. His mind was still processing the situation.

"Sure, Cole. Lead the way."

I headed outside the saloon and into an alley between that place and a gun store. Johnny still looked as if he didn't want to talk to me. It was also another very normal reaction, given that men didn't have the habit of meeting in alleys for chit-chatting.

"Your belly still looks huge, Cole. Drinking too much lately?" Johnny asked. He was cracking a joke to make the situation feel less heavy on him. He always liked to do that in the most inopportune situations, which was something I didn't like about him.

"This isn't the moment to make jokes, Johnny."

He looked serious once again.

"My belly is this huge not because I drink too much. I'm pregnant, Johnny. And yes, I know how ridiculous that sounds. And stop staring at me with that face. It makes me want to punch you."

His face was that of someone who was thinking that maybe he was dreaming.

"Am I dreaming? Is this a nightmare?" Johnny asked before he pinched himself.

"Nope, definitely not dreaming," he answered to himself.

I couldn't stand that silly reaction from him; it infuriated me. I grabbed him by his shirt and slammed the young man against the wall of the saloon.

"Look here, do you think I'm joking? Why do you think I have this big belly that doesn't want to go away? I'm pregnant and the father is you. There, I said it. You can start screaming or make another silly joke. I don't care anymore."

I left him there and walked away. I didn't know where I was going. I just wanted to be away from Johnny.

CHAPTER 4

Hours after meeting Johnny, I got home and sat on the couch. I closed my eyes and began to breathe in and out slowly. I needed to think things through. I needed to relax.

I heard someone knocking on the door. I didn't care who it was. I pretended I wasn't home and let the person keep on knocking.

Then, I heard Johnny's voice, "Cole, it's me, Johnny. Let me in. I'm sorry I didn't take you seriously."

I didn't respond to him immediately; I was still pissed at the young man. Then, I got up and opened the door.

"Fine, come in, jerk."

We sat on opposite couches. I looked at him and he looked at me. We stayed like that for a couple of seconds until he broke the silence, "So, you're pregnant? That's why your belly is so big?"

I sighed and said, "Yes, that's what I tried telling you before you made me angry with your bad jokes."

"Sorry about that, but I can't help it. What really happened and how are you sure I'm the father?"

I explained to him my quest to find an explanation for my pregnancy. He seemed to take it well and looked a bit happy. It was definitely not what I expected from someone as immature as

Johnny.

"Well, Cole, that's just how it is. I'm willing to father that baby. I know how this place is and how my parents would react, which is why we should keep this secret from them."

Wow, where did all that matureness come from all of a sudden? Did I really not know him well, after all?

Johnny was a box full of surprises. One moment he was capable of making me want to kill him, and other times he made me want to slap that ass and plunge into his hole with my cock. There was no middle ground with him.

"Well, it looks like we are going to have to live together, Cole," Johnny affirmed, smiling.

I felt something I hadn't felt in months. I missed that feeling. I wanted a man to take me and make me his. The first time we met, Johnny was so good at that.

The young man got up from the chair and sat on my lap. I felt my cock growing huge. Johnny looked at my bulge and grinned.

"I missed you," Johnny purred while caressing my crotch.

I closed my eyes and felt his lips approaching mine. We kissed. I felt how passionate he was. Maybe the feeling of becoming a father had transformed him. Perhaps it turned that guy into a real man.

He had already deflowered me before. His cock, which was long and fat as fuck, was like a dream come true. The amount of man milk he could unload… Jesus, the first time it happened it was almost too much to take.

I felt my heart racing, my blood getting hotter. My cock was growing bigger in my pants. Johnny was the perfect partner when he wanted to be. He was just so good when he was in the right mood!

I put my hand on his back and began to caress it. It felt strong and confident. He wanted me. He wanted to impregnate me again if he could. I could feel his muscles getting tense and flexing.

"Time to get yourself ready, cowboy," Johnny joked and his

words melted my heart. *Goddammit, he could be so sexy sometimes.*

"I'm all yours. Make me your bitch like last time..." I purred and the young man smirked. Every time I heard his soft words, I wanted him to take me to bed and undress me.

That's what he did. He picked me up with ease in his skinny – yet strong – arms and took me to my bed. He was dominating me in my own house and I was letting him do it.

He kissed me on the way there, and he was caring and lovely. I never thought he was already so mature.

There I was, a forty-year-old grown-up acting like a boy in front of someone years younger than me.

Life and my feelings were funny sometimes, and I couldn't care less. I loved being dominated by someone much younger than me.

Johnny put me on the bed carefully and began to undress me. First, he took off my boots and socks. He began to suck on my toes, one by one. *He was just so proficient at that!*

His tongue racing around the skin down there, his warm lips devouring my fingers, it was so good I couldn't stay quiet. I began to moan and groan like we'd done this plenty of times before. The real action had barely started and Johnny was already claiming me, making me submit.

"Just keep going, Johnny. Make me yours today", I said as I groaned. The younger man smirked and caressed my forehead, showing me that he heard me.

The young man took off my pants and I noticed that he was ogling my big bulge. I had a big cock and a heavy sack, but I really liked being the submissive one in our sex. I wanted Johnny to suck on my dick fervently, but not right now. He had to love my legs first.

I felt his strong hands on my legs. I could feel how much he wanted me. I was so lucky to have this man with me. He was going to be the perfect father and I was going to be a good mother.

Yes, yes, a mother, that's who I want to become. First, though, I need to leave the village so that we can live peacefully in a better place. Maybe north, where people are more receptive of man-on-man love. Yes, maybe there, but I have other things to take care of at the moment. Johnny can't stop thinking about making me his bitch again.

I felt Johnny's tongue sucking and racing over the skin of my legs. He was just so good at that! He was getting a feel for my body, probing me for what I was really like. It was all just preparation for the real action later. Johnny was learning everything he could so that he could impale me perfectly with his fat cock.

"I'm still getting ready, Cole. Be patient."

His tongue finally reached the underside of my bulge. He put his big mouth there and began to suck on my lump. It didn't matter if the underwear was still there – he was going to play with my junk regardless.

I imagined he didn't want to suck my cock right then and there. Why delay something so good, though? Sometimes, I couldn't understand him.

Yes, yes, let's take it slow and nice. Make me your woman today, Johnny. Make me your slut like last time.

He put his hand on my bulge and began to massage it nicely. My cock was growing bigger. It was almost completely hard. It was almost ready for him to suck it off.

Johnny put his big hands on my asscheeks and lifted my butt off the bed. Then, he put his head down there and let the weight of my body fall onto his boyish face. He began to suck my hole and lick the skin down there.

The young man was naughty and didn't feel ashamed. When he was in the right mood, nothing could stand in his way. He wanted to make sure I was going to get the best from him.

There I was, a pregnant old man getting dominated and acting like a defenseless woman in my own bed. I could feel the weight of my belly and the baby inside of it, and it turned me on more than I already was. What's better than being pregnant and getting fucked at the same time? I envied that women could get pregnant and that it was expected of them.

Being pregnant and having sex, it's what life is really about!

Johnny pulled his body up, positioning himself underneath me. Our lips were almost touching and I could feel the minty aroma coming out of his mouth. I wanted to kiss his hot red lips, but I couldn't. I couldn't stop groaning.

The young man's hands were probing my anus. He added a finger, then the next, and then one more. What a proficient young man he was!

I could only moan in pleasure. I was feeling so happy to have someone like him as my future husband. And yes, we were going to marry eventually.

The young cowboy put his hands on the sides of my torso and moved them up and down. He did it so slowly and nicely that I could feel each finger loving me.

The man knew how to get me in the right mood. I closed my eyes and let my feelings take over my body.

Johnny put his head under my armpit and began to sniff it, "It's hairy and smelly. I love it."

Goddammit, that voice and the way he said it, I could only get so hard. The foreplay was nice, but I was getting impatient. I wanted him all over my shaft right now.

I shoved my underwear down, my cock jumping out and bouncing up and down, eager for some man-on-man action.

"Fuck me, Johnny, and suck my cock. Do it like it happened last time. I want to feel your wet mouth on my dick."

"On it", the young cowboy exclaimed.

In a matter of seconds, he positioned himself in front of me and began to suck on my cock. He put my big mushroom head in first and I could feel the way his lips worked on it. I was getting so turned on and ready to blow my load I knew I wasn't going to last much longer.

The cowboy, then, put one inch after another inch into his

mouth. I could feel his hungry mouth devouring my rod. He was doing it so effortlessly that I asked myself if he hadn't had other experiences after we broke up. Wouldn't be surprised if my lover played with other men before I stumbled on him in the saloon earlier today.

Finally, Johnny was deep-throating me. My cock was pulsating in his mouth. He looked at me, our eyes locking with each other. I saw him grinning before he continued his amazing work. The look on his face meant that he was almost there. He wanted to let me know that I could blow in his mouth anytime.

I groaned and moaned. Johnny went up and down, up and down, sometimes slow, sometimes really fast. The cowboy knew how to make me feel like a slut.

Eventually, I felt my orgasm coming. It started in my cockhead before sweeping through my body. My muscles bulged and I knew that the moment I was waiting for was coming.

Johnny grinned and began to swallow my load, his eyes looking hungry for more and more. One gulp after the other, he still looked thirsty. He had quite the appetite. He swallowed every rope, not even taking a break to catch his breath. *Holy shit, I couldn't believe Johnny was so good at this! I wish I were like him sometimes...*

The young cowboy said, "Think I've done a good job with your cock. Time for you to spread your legs for me, love."

I remembered the first time he rammed me with his dick. He was a couple of months older than 18 and already had a shaft so fat I couldn't believe he was its owner. I was envious.

Johnny could read the fear in my eyes, which was a very natural reaction. The last time he penetrated me, the last time he was inside of me, it was so painful that I barely felt any satisfaction.

I still wanted to have him ramming my non-virgin ass again, but I was hoping that this time it was going to be different. I knew how much I could enjoy that and I wanted every little bit of it.

"Don't worry, Cole. This time, I'll take it easy on you. You can't get pregnant twice, right? Although... I'd love to make another baby with you."

He was going to ram my ass like the bull he was, and I was going to let him take me to the heavens.

"You forgot my shirt. You didn't take it off yet," I ordered.

"On it," the cowboy said. I was still on the bed. He climbed up on me, legs between my torso, and then took off my shirt. I felt his manliness surrounding me and his musky smell in my nose. There was also something else in the air... the smell of horses, farms, animals, and dirt, and that really turned me on.

Then, Johnny began to get undressed. He took his shirt off, then his pants and his underwear. The boots were the last thing to go. I cherished his skinny body on top of me. I put my hand on his back and felt the smoothness of his skin.

So young and perfect...

"I want you inside of me. I want to feel your seed again," I purred and he smirked. He must have felt proud of himself at that moment that he was dominating a man so much older and bigger than him.

We began to make out again. I felt his tongue all over mine, his lips caressing mine. He was the hottest man in the village and was making sure I always remembered that.

The full length of his cock was on my belly. His seed was inside of me, his fat shaft settled on my big belly. Thinking about that really turned me on again and I felt my cock growing bigger for the second time in a row.

I slapped his ass a couple of times as I told him what I wanted. I spread my legs even wider for him and he positioned himself in front of my hole.

My big belly was one of my most noticeable features at that moment. Johnny caressed it and said, "I'll do this slowly and make sure neither you nor the little one is hurt this time."

I could only groan and moan at those words.

So hot, so alpha, and so dominating. He was my favorite little devil.

Johnny began his handiwork on my hole with his tongue. I felt how wet and cold it was. I could only groan more and more. He raced his tongue around my orifice before giving it a nice kiss.

Then, he grabbed his fat cock and aimed it where my hole was. He closed one eye and pretended that he was a sharpshooter. I almost laughed at that moment. Johnny sure had a weird sense of humor.

"I want to do something else first," the young man said. Confused, I almost asked him what it was, but I decided I didn't want to spoil the surprise.

He climbed up on me again and positioned his juicy cock on top of my pregnant belly. Then, he began to pound in and out with his mighty, fat cock.

Holy shit, Johnny sure gets some crazy ideas from time to time. I almost burst out laughing, but I was feeling too much sexual pleasure to do that. The world around me looked foggy and I welcomed it.

"This little one right here - he's mine! I'm his father and proud of it."

Jesus, could he be any more perfect? I felt so safe around him. I couldn't help but wonder the type of man he'd become, a few years from now...

Thinking about that made me want to have Johnny all for myself for the rest of my life. Maybe we were going to get that.

Finally, Johnny was ready to ram my ass. He put his gigantic cockhead in and I felt a bit of pain. I felt the little one moving a bit. He was feeling a little uncomfortable, but that was okay. He was safe inside of me.

I put a hand on the belly and calmed them down, "Shh, shh, shh, don't worry. He's your father and he'll take care of you. We love you very much."

At that moment, I realized that I hadn't thought of choosing a name for the baby. Well, it would have to wait until I was done with Johnny.

I felt the first thrust from the young cowboy. The cock went all the way in and hit my prostate. There was some pain once again, but it was a lot less than last time. My rectum got used to his size. I wished I had more experience with gay sex so that I could make this even better than it was.

Then came another thrust, and I felt no more pain, just pleasure and the feeling of wanting this moment to last forever.

Johnny kept on going, ramming me with all of his might. He had so much energy. He couldn't stop, not even for a second to catch his breath. He rammed and rammed me continuously. I kept on groaning as loudly as I could.

I didn't care if the villagers were going to hear us this time. I was enjoying this magical moment so much. My life mattered more than theirs.

"You are as hot and tight as the last time, Cole," Johnny remarked, already looking a bit exhausted. I wasn't surprised that he was. It had already been a couple of minutes since he started eating me bareback.

"I'm almost there", the young man groaned before I felt his body growing tense. His cock began to throb uncontrollably and I felt the first wave of his man milk coming out in my hole.

I groaned, following his rhythm. It happened in waves in the beginning, but then the cumming turned into a pure stream. I saw some of his milk dripping onto the bedsheets.

What a shame I wasn't going to manage to keep it all inside of me.

Then, Johnny took one last breath before he plopped down on the bed, being by my side. I felt the usual smell of cum in the air. The young man had had so much honey in him. It was incredible seeing him releasing everything in me like that.

"That was so fucking good", Johnny moaned before he smiled. I smiled back. We remained there on the bed for a couple of minutes, staring at each other before we fell asleep.

CHAPTER 5

I woke up to the sound of noises outside the house. I was groggy as hell and Johnny was still asleep. What was going on outside? I could barely understand what it was that people were shouting and yelling about.

Then, I heard something along the lines of "…those two were having sex! That's a sin! They need to be killed or else the whole village will be cursed!"

Shit, they found out about Johnny and me.

I slapped my lover in the face gently and he woke up instantly. He sat up on the bed quickly, looking as groggy as I was.

"Johnny, we need to go! Everyone's found out about us. I have a horse outside. We can sneak out through the backdoor and leave the village. Do you want to come with me?"

He studied me for a couple of seconds before responding, "Of course. Let's go!"

There was very little time to think about the consequences of Johnny leaving his parents behind or anything else, for that matter, so none of us mentioned anything that could delay our escape.

Johnny and I were still fully naked. The villagers were trying to break into my home. I heard them pounding against the door and trying to break the windows. *Holy shit, they were losing their mind over two men loving each other.*

I threw my clothes back on, yanking up my pants. I felt some nausea, but I managed to quench it. Adrenaline was in every part of my body. I helped Johnny get dressed however I could, putting his shirt and pants on him.

I grabbed some of my stuff and shoved it into a bag. I made sure to get some extra clothes since Johnny was going to need them later, and then we headed to the backdoor.

I threw it open and noticed that my horse was still in the stable.

Perfect, so those idiots didn't try getting Artax yet!

Johnny was just behind me and we sat on the horse as quickly as we could. I heard some villagers coming from the sides of the house when I took a shortcut to the main road. Gladly, I was too far from them already, but I did see some tree branches and rocks being thrown at us.

Once we were so far from the village that nobody from there could chase us anymore, I stopped the horse so that we could catch our breaths. I left Artax by a tree and sat down with Johnny in a forest.

"That was too close", Johnny said.

"Yeah, definitely", I said, "so, do you really understand what this means? Seeing your parents again will be very difficult."

"Well, I haven't given that much thought yet. I can, however, send my parents some letters to explain to them what happened. If they do understand that I love you, then I could meet up with them again… sometime. I was never close to them, though, you know? I don't think I will miss them much."

Well, at least that was a problem I didn't have to worry about. Johnny was okay with leaving his parents behind and living with me.

I put my arm over his shoulders and let the young cowboy rest his body on mine. He was warm and made me feel calmer, the sun bright in the cyan-blue sky.

"So, where are we going now, love?" Johnny asked.

I thought about my answer. There was a place I could go to. My friend in the north had a very big house and he wouldn't have a problem letting us live with him for a while. He liked men too, so that could be a bonus later on.

"To the north. We will go to a city called Great Falls. It will take us a couple of hours to get there, but we should be there by midnight. What do you think?"

Johnny glanced at me and I saw how much he loved me. His eyes showed that he wanted only the best for us.

"Of course, wherever you want us to go."

He rested his head on my chest and I caressed his head. The days ahead were going to be difficult, but with him by my side, I felt like I could beat any obstacle.

The End

The next page has a HOT Mpreg romance sneak peek. Go check it out! And leave a review if you liked the book. It always helps me so much!

SNEAK PEEK: OVERWHELMING THE OMEGA

An Omegaverse MPREG Story (Lost Innocence - 1)

"Come on, Justin. It's yours if you want it," he said. His words were almost inaudible, though I didn't know if it was because of me, given the state of my mind, or because he was losing himself as well.

Slowly, but surely, I moved my shaking hand to his cock. It stood hovering above it for a few seconds before I dared to wrap my fingers around it. The moment they were locked around his big man tool, I sensed the thing throb slightly. Moments after, it was already growing in size.

His cock was warm - more so than the ambient air. It was so inviting to touch something so soft and tender. And I as I moved my hand a bit, I was rewarded by his toy growing a little bit. His balls moved when the side of my hand touched the skin of his sac. They went down a couple of inches, indicating the Hugo was getting in the mood.

Even though things had barely started, I moaned. My hand

moved up and down on his shaft. I was doing it slowly not to spook myself. I had no idea how big his toy could get. I also had no idea how loose his balls could be.

His shaft was not in a semi-solid state, though it was evident already that it would be too much for me. My fingers were never going to grip the whole thing.

As it continued to grow thicker, my fingers were forced to open up more space for its veiny surface to expand. It had now such a striking girth that my thumb lost its contact with my other fingers.

All the while, I continued to give him a handjob, not caring one bit that fear was still taking hold of me. I wanted to be calm in that situation, but it was simply impossible while my sight was more and more dominated by his growing package.

His shaft was now fully hard. It was so big that I had to blink twice. My poor mind could not grasp that such a thing existed.

"Suck it," he said, and I didn't need another invitation. My head moved down on the same instant, with my heart still pounding out of fear.

The moment I wrapped my lips around his bulbous cockhead, I knew that was what I had been born for. An Omega in heat like me just needed some good dick to worship before starting a day. My job had already started, but who's to say Hugo would not want me to come back, especially if he liked the blowjob?

Or flip to the next page for more stories like this one.

MPREG SERIES AND MORE

SERIES - PREGNANT FOR HIM

1. Controlled by the Alpha 1: An MPREG Omegaverse Story
2. Controlled by the Alpha 2: An MPREG Omegaverse Story
3. Controlled by the Alpha 3: Dominating the Fertile Omega
4. Controlled by the Alpha 4: An Omega's Tale of Obedience
5. Controlled by the Alpha 5: A Tale of Obedient Submission
6. Controlled by the Alpha 6: Monopolized in Outer Space

SERIES - LOST INNOCENCE

1. Overwhelming the Omega 1: His Little Doll
2. Overwhelming the Omega 2: Brute Entry and Double Teamed
3. Overwhelming the Omega 3: His Tight Backdoor
4. Overwhelming the Omega 4: Stretching his Front Door
5. Overwhelming the Omega 5: Until he Spasms
6. Overwhelming the Omega 6: Naïve and Untouched

SERIES - FERAL NEEDS

1. Tasting the Omega 1: Rock-Hard
2. Tasting the Omega 2: Reckless Entry

3. Tasting the Omega 3: Rough in Public

4. Tasting the Omega 4: So Big It Hurts

Straight to gay first time bundles:

1. Stuffed by Blue Collars: The Full Straight to Gay Age Gap Story

2. Throbbing Hard: A Straight to Gay MMF Bundle

3. Teasing Older Men: 16 Straight to Gay MM Stories

4. Helping Hand: 13 Forbidden Older Man Stories

5. So BIG It Hurts MEGA Bundle: 14 Stories of Man of the House, Brats and Gay Sitters

ABOUT THE AUTHOR

Michael Levi's biggest passion? Writing steamy, romantic stories that leave his readers panting. He's currently focusing on ABDL MM romances, but his collection is diverse and there are books for everyone's tastes. If you're looking for straight to gay, first time, BBC, sissification, and more, you're going to find them on his author page.

He lives to pamper his readers, every kiss means a lot more than what meets the eye, and he loves his Alpha males. Making sure that every gay first time feels different, Michael Levi writes his stories with a cup of coffee by his side. And for inspiration, he always opens a photo of his new crush.